The Voyages of Doctor Dolittle

Retold from the Hugh Lofting original by Kathleen Olmstead

Illustrated by Lucy Corvino

STERLING

New York / London
www.sterlingpublishing.com/kids

STERLING and the distinctive Sterling logo
are registered trademarks of Sterling Publishing Co., Inc.

Library of Congress Cataloging-in-Publication Data

Olmstead, Kathleen.
 The voyages of Doctor Dolittle / retold from the Hugh Lofting original ;
abridged by Kathleen Olmstead ; illustrated by Lucy Corvino ; afterword
by Arthur Pober.
  p. cm.—(Classic starts)
 Summary: An abridged retelling of the story in which Dr. Dolittle sets off
with his assistant, Tommy Stubbins, his dog, Jip, and Polynesia the parrot on
an adventurous voyage over tropical seas to floating Spidermonkey Island.
 ISBN-13: 978-1-4027-4574-4 (alk. paper)
 ISBN-10: 1-4027-4574-5 (alk. paper)
 [1. Animals—Fiction. 2. Fantasy.] I. Corvino, Lucy, ill. II. Lofting, Hugh,
1886–1947. Voyages of Doctor Dolittle. III. Title.

PZ7.O499Vo 2008
[Fic]—dc22

2007003735

2 4 6 8 10 9 7 5 3 1

Published by Sterling Publishing Co., Inc.
387 Park Avenue South, New York, NY 10016
Copyright © 2008 by Kathleen Olmstead
Illustrations copyright © 2008 by Lucy Corvino
Distributed in Canada by Sterling Publishing
c/o Canadian Manda Group, 165 Dufferin Street,
Toronto, Ontario, Canada M6K 3H6
Distributed in the United Kingdom by GMC Distribution Services,
Castle Place, 166 High Street, Lewes, East Sussex, England BN7 1XU
Distributed in Australia by Capricorn Link (Australia) Pty. Ltd.
P.O. Box 704, Windsor, NSW 2756, Australia

Classic Starts is a trademark of Sterling Publishing Co., Inc.

Printed in China
All rights reserved

Sterling ISBN-13: 978-1-4027-4574-4
ISBN-10: 1-4027-4574-5

For information about custom editions, special sales, premium and
corporate purchases, please contact Sterling Special Sales
Department at 800-805-5489 or specialsales@sterlingpub.com.

CONTENTS

CHAPTER 1

Puddleby

∽

A great many years ago, there lived a doctor called Dolittle. This was long before your grandfathers were little boys or your grandmothers were little girls. His full name was John Dolittle, MD. The *MD* showed that he was a proper doctor. He was a very smart man who helped many sick people.

Doctor Dolittle lived in a very small town called Puddleby-on-the-Marsh. Everyone in town knew him. After all, he was easy to recognize. He was a tall man and always wore a high hat. This made him look even taller. He also wore a long black coat with deep pockets. Doctor Dolittle kept many things in these pockets: a handkerchief, an apple in case he ran into a horse, and a notebook.

Whenever he walked down Main Street, people would point and say, "Look! There goes the doctor! He's such a clever man." Children ran after him, laughing and asking questions. Doctor Dolittle always answered them. He never thought a question was silly.

Dogs would wag their tails and follow him down the street. Even the crows who lived in the church tower would fly over him, cawing to him and nodding.

Doctor Dolittle lived in a little house at the edge of town. The house was small, but his garden was large. There was a lot of grass and many trees. A low wall surrounded his yard. There were many shady resting places. His sister Sarah lived with him. She took care of the house, and Doctor Dolittle took care of the garden.

He also kept a lot of pets. Doctor Dolittle was very fond of animals, you see. There were goldfish in the pond at the bottom of his garden. He had rabbits in a little hutch beside his house. White mice lived in his piano. A squirrel stayed in his linen cabinet, and there was a hedgehog in the cellar. He even kept a cow as a pet.

The cow and her calf shared the shed with an old horse. This horse had lived with Doctor Dolittle for more than twenty-five years, so they were quite good friends. There were chickens and pigeons, two lambs, a goat, and many other animals living in the same yard. His favorite pets, though, were Dab-Dab the duck, Jip the dog, Gub-Gub the pig, Polynesia the parrot, and Too-Too the owl.

His sister Sarah often complained about the animals. It was hard to keep a tidy house with so many animals running around, she said. It made it difficult for the doctor's patients when they came for appointments.

One day, an old woman came in for a checkup and sat down on the hedgehog. He was sound asleep on the sofa and did not hear her come in. The poor woman was so surprised that she screamed and ran back out the door. She vowed never to see Doctor Dolittle again. Instead, she drove to a town ten miles away to see another doctor. Sarah Dolittle decided it was time to speak to her brother about his animals.

"John," she said, "how can you expect your patients to visit with so many animals in the house?" She placed her hands on her hips and spoke sternly. "That's the fourth patient the animals have driven away. Mr. Jenkins says that he won't come back. Even the minister has had enough! We cannot afford to lose any more. If you

keep this up, we will lose all our best patients."
Sarah was really quite angry.

"But I like the animals better than our best
patients," said the doctor.

"You are ridiculous," said his sister. Then she
walked out of the room.

As time went on, the good doctor got more
and more animals. More animals meant fewer
people came to see him. Eventually he had only
one patient—the butcher.

The butcher did not mind being around all
the animals but he only got sick once a year. This
was not enough money for Doctor Dolittle and
his sister to pay all their bills. Also, there were a
lot of animals to feed!

The doctor had some money saved. It could
have lasted years, but he kept bringing home
more animals. So he moved the white mice into a
dresser drawer and sold the piano. Then he sold

his brown suit. He sold a wagon and some books and an old table from the kitchen. Still there was too little money and too many animals. Doctor Dolittle and his sister became poorer and poorer.

When he walked down the street in his high hat, the grown-ups pointed to him. They said, "There goes Doctor Dolittle! He used to be the best-known doctor in the county. Now he's too poor to own a good suit. He hasn't any money, and his stockings are full of holes!"

Doctor Dolittle paid no attention. He was still a happy man.

And the dogs and cats and children still ran after him. The dogs still wagged their tails and the children still asked questions. As always, the good doctor took his time to talk to them all.

CHAPTER 2

Animal Language

⌒

One day, the butcher stopped by for a visit. He noticed that the doctor's coat had several patches. The butcher knew that he was doctor's only patient. He knew Doctor Dolittle and his sister must be very poor with so little income. The butcher looked around the kitchen and noticed all the animals. They all looked happy and healthy. Suddenly the butcher had an idea.

"I know!" he exclaimed. "Why don't you stop being a people doctor and start being an animal doctor?"

Polynesia the parrot was sitting on the windowsill singing a song to herself. When she heard the butcher say this, she stopped to listen.

"It makes perfect sense," the butcher continued. "You know everything about animals. I'm sure you know a lot more than most animal doctors. I've noticed that you get along with animals better than people. I don't mean that you don't get along with people, of course. It's just that you seem more relaxed with animals. And they're very relaxed around you. Look at your kitchen! It's filled with happy animals!"

It was true. Jip the dog and Gub-Gub the pig were curled up together in a corner. Dab-Dab the duck sat on the counter cleaning her feathers. The hedgehog was beneath the table taking a nap. The mice were playing in a box by the door. Polynesia the parrot, as you know, sat on the windowsill listening to every word.

"Well, I don't know," Doctor Dolittle said. "I hadn't thought of that before. Seems like such a strange idea."

"Strange?" the butcher exclaimed. "Why, it makes perfect sense! There are so many farmers around here with cows and sheep who could use your help. Plus, there are all the cats and dogs in town. Animals get sick just as often as people. Trust me," he said. "You should be an animal doctor!"

After the butcher left, Polynesia flew from her perch and sat beside Doctor Dolittle. "That man has a lot of sense," she said. "You should be an animal doctor. Those people were silly to stop coming here. You are the best doctor in the world. The animals need you."

"Oh, there are plenty of animal doctors around," Doctor Dolittle said. He shook his head and gave a little chuckle. He got up from the table and started to clear the dishes.

"Yes, there are plenty," said Polynesia. "But you would be the best. I'm certain that there would be no other animal doctor who could compete with you."

Polynesia flew back to the windowsill where Doctor Dolittle was now fixing some flowerpots. "I'm going to tell you something very important, so I want you to listen carefully," she said.

Doctor Dolittle put the flowerpot down and turned to look at the parrot.

"Did you know that animals can talk?" she asked.

"I know that parrots can talk, of course," he said with a smile.

"Yes, we parrots can talk in two languages—human language and bird language," Polynesia said proudly. "If I say, 'Polly wants a cracker,' you understand me. Now, listen to this: *Ka-ka o-ee, fee-fee?*"

"My word!" cried the doctor. "What on earth does that mean?"

"That means, 'Is the tea ready?' in bird language," she said. She nodded a few times and bounced on the windowsill. It was exciting to share this information with the doctor. She wondered why she had not thought of it before.

"You don't say!" he exclaimed. "That is so interesting! I've never heard you speak that way before."

"Well, why would I?" Polynesia asked. "You never would have understood me. There really isn't much point talking like that in front of people. That's why we usually keep it all to ourselves."

"Tell me more," said the doctor. He was excited by this news. "No, wait!" He pulled his notebook and pencil from his pocket. "Now, don't go too fast and I'll write it all down."

He sat back down at the table. "Let's start at the beginning. Tell me the birds' alphabet." And so their lessons began.

That was how Doctor Dolittle learned the animals have their own language and can talk to one another. All that afternoon, he sat in the kitchen with Polynesia learning the words in the bird language. He carefully wrote down each one in his notebook. He spelled them out the way they sounded so he would remember later.

A few hours later, Jip the dog woke up. He walked over to Polynesia and the doctor. "See?" Polynesia said. "He's talking to you."

"I didn't hear anything," Doctor Dolittle said. "I only noticed him scratching his ear."

"Animals don't always speak with sounds," she replied. "We talk with our ears, our feet, our tails—we use every part of our bodies to talk. Sometimes we don't want to make a noise. Do you see how he's twitching with one side of his nose?"

"Yes, yes, I see that!" Doctor Dolittle said. "What does it mean?"

"He's asking you if you've noticed that it stopped raining," Polynesia said. "Dogs nearly always use their noses to ask questions." The doctor quickly wrote this information down, too.

It did not take long before Doctor Dolittle could understand and speak to the animals himself. He still needed Polynesia's help sometimes, but he was confident he would soon be able to converse on his own. This is when he finally decided to take the butcher's advice. He stopped being a human doctor and started treating animals instead.

CHAPTER 3

Success at Last!

⌒

The butcher helped spread the word. Soon everyone knew that Doctor Dolittle was now helping animals. Old ladies brought their poodles who had eaten too much cake. Farmers traveled many miles to bring him sick cows and sheep. Children carried their cats with the sniffles. Doctor Dolittle had many new patients, and he was a very happy man.

One day a plow horse was brought to him. The poor thing was glad to find a man who could talk to him. It had been so hard for him not being understood.

"You know, Doctor," the horse said, "the first vet they took me to knew nothing at all. For the past six weeks, he has been giving me medicine for headaches. What I really need is glasses! I'm going blind in one eye."

Doctor Dolittle looked carefully into the horse's left eye. It was indeed cloudy. "I can make you some glasses right away," he said.

"I'd like some just like yours," the horse said. "Except I would like green glass in mine. That will help block the sun when I am working in the field."

"Of course," Doctor Dolittle replied. "Green ones you shall have!"

He led the plow horse to the door of his office. "I'll have them ready for you next week," he said.

"You know, Doctor," the horse said as he

walked out the door, "the trouble with most vets is that they think everything they do is correct because the animals don't complain."

"I'm a pretty quiet creature as a rule," the horse continued. "I'm usually patient with people. It's just so difficult when they are clearly paying no attention. I'm afraid that I sometimes lose my temper."

"We must all try to be patient," the good doctor said. "You should try to remember that most people mean well."

Doctor Dolittle patted the horse on the back and sent him on his way. When the horse returned a week later, the doctor gave him a big pair of green glasses.

As you might imagine, people were surprised to see a horse wearing glasses. Whenever he was in the field working, people stopped and stared. However, they were not surprised to learn the glasses came from Doctor Dolittle. It was just the

kind of thing they were coming to expect from him. It wasn't long before it was common to see a horse wearing glasses. Then there were dogs wearing casts and a cat walking with a crutch. There was a cow wearing a neck brace and a goat wearing a monocle.

All these animals were so happy with Doctor Dolittle that they told other animals. Word spread from one county to the next. Creatures everywhere were excited to learn that an animal doctor could understand their language. He would listen to them and help them with any problem.

Wild animals heard about Doctor Dolittle, too. Many came in from the forest to see him. Badgers, bats, squirrels, wolves, owls, and foxes all gathered in his yard. Eventually, there were so many animals that Doctor Dolittle had to organize them all.

He made special signs to go above doors for the different kinds of animals. He wrote HORSES over the front door, COWS over the side door, and SHEEP over the kitchen door. Even the mice had their own tiny entrance by the cellar. This made things much easier for the doctor. He could then go see the animals as they lined up patiently by their door.

Doctor Dolittle's life continued like this for several years. Animals from miles around came to Puddleby-on-the-Marsh to see him. In this way he became famous among the animals all over the world. Doctor Dolittle was happy, and he liked his life very much.

One day, Polynesia sat on her usual perch at the window. She was looking outside. Suddenly she began to laugh.

"Whatever is so funny?" Doctor Dolittle asked. He had been reading the morning paper and was surprised by the bird's laughter.

"I was just thinking that people are so funny," she said. "They spend so much time with animals but the only thing they've learned is that a dog wagging his tail means he's happy."

"And that made you laugh?" the doctor asked.

"I think it's funny that you're the first one to try to understand us. After all these years, someone finally took the time to understand." Polynesia shook her head laughing.

"Well, I suppose that is strange," Doctor Dolittle said.

"I knew a macaw once who could say 'Good morning' in seven different human languages. An old professor taught him," Polynesia said. "But my friend was frustrated. He said the old man didn't speak Greek properly. He wanted to correct him but worried that it might be rude."

Polynesia suddenly looked serious. She turned to Doctor Dolittle and said, "There are so many things that people can't do. They can't fly. They can't stay underwater for long periods of time. They can't run as fast as a cart or a train. Yet they still think they are better than everything else around them. Why is that?"

"I'm sorry," the doctor said sadly. "I don't know the answer to that question. I've often wondered the very same thing."

CHAPTER 4

More Money Troubles

~~

Doctor Dolittle and the animals were not the only ones happy with his new business. His sister Sarah was also pleased. At long last they had money coming into the household. She even bought a new dress to wear on Sundays. The animals still upset her, though. It was impossible to keep a clean house.

Some of the animal patients were so sick that they had to stay a week. They would sit on chairs on the lawn or relax in the garden. And too often when the animals were feeling better, they did not want to leave. They liked staying with Doctor Dolittle too much. The doctor never had the heart to say no. So the number of pets at his house grew and grew.

One day while he was walking through town, he saw an organ-grinder with a monkey on a string. Right away, the doctor noticed that the monkey's collar was on too tight. He could see that the little animal was unhappy. So he gave the man a dollar and took the monkey away from him. At first, the organ grinder was angry. He did not want to give up the monkey. But Doctor Dolittle said he would call the police and report his cruelty. The man realized he had lost the argument. He took his dollar and left.

So the monkey moved in with Doctor Dolittle and all his pets. The other animals named him Chee-Chee, which means "ginger" in monkey language.

On another day, the circus came to town. A crocodile traveling with the circus had a bad toothache. He escaped in the middle of the night and went to Doctor Dolittle. The doctor could speak to him in crocodile language, of course. He took the crocodile into his house and fixed the sore tooth. As you might imagine, the crocodile did not want to leave. He asked the doctor if he could live by the pond at the end of the garden if he promised not to eat the fish. Of course, the doctor could not refuse. The crocodile kept his word. He was always quiet and gentle with everyone in the house. When the circus men came to take the crocodile back, they saw that he was happy and calm. They agreed with the doctor that the crocodile would be much happier staying there, so they left him behind.

However, the doctor's sister Sarah was not happy. She was frightened of the crocodile. She worried that other people would be frightened, too. Unfortunately, she was right. The old ladies stopped bringing their sick poodles. They were afraid the crocodile would eat their beloved pets. The farmers stopped bringing their sheep for the same reason.

Doctor Dolittle tried talking to the crocodile. He explained that he was losing patients because people were afraid. The doctor told the crocodile that he would have to go back to the circus. The crocodile wept big tears and begged the doctor let him stay. Of course, the doctor agreed. He could not stand to see an unhappy animal.

"This is the last straw," his sister said. "We were just starting to do well again. We will be in the poorhouse again in no time. That alligator must go!"

"It's not an alligator," Doctor Dolittle calmly replied. "It's a crocodile."

"I don't care what it is," his sister said. "It's an awful thing to find under a bed."

"He has promised me that he won't hurt any animal," said the doctor. "I trust him completely."

"Trust him?" she screamed. "Have you gone mad? People have stopped coming because of that creature. I've had enough. Either he goes or I do."

So that was that. Doctor Dolittle's sister Sarah packed up her things and left. She moved to the next street and took a job as a housekeeper. Eventually she married a very nice man and lived a quiet and happy life. As you might suspect, her house was always neat and tidy.

Although Doctor Dolittle was very happy with his animals, it was still a difficult time. His sister was right: People were afraid of the crocodile. He lost most of his patients. Once again, the doctor had very little money. Also, without his sister, there was no one else to help around the house. He could not afford to hire help, so the animals did their best to pitch in.

Chee-Chee the monkey did all the cooking and sewing. Too-Too the owl helped with the household accounts. He was good with arithmetic, you see. Dab-Dab the duck dusted and made the beds. Gub-Gub the pig helped with the garden. And Polynesia became the housekeeper. This meant that she was in charge of the whole household. She made sure that everything was done properly.

It took some time before the animals could do their jobs. Watching Jip the dog sweep the floor with his tail was very amusing! They were all determined to make it work, though. They tried and tried until they could do it perfectly. It was the least they could do for the doctor who had given so much to them.

Money continued to be a problem, however. There were so many mouths to feed and so few patients bringing in money. So the animals set up a little stall at the side of the road. They sold vegetables from the garden. If Polynesia worried about not having enough money to buy fish for dinner, Doctor Dolittle just shrugged.

"You shouldn't worry so much," he said. "You sound like my sister. As long as the chickens lay eggs and the cows give milk, we will be fine. We can always make omelets for dinner. Besides, winter is a long way off. We'll have time to make more money."

But winter came much earlier than expected that year. There were no more vegetables from the garden. They had a nice big fire to sit around, but the animals were hungry. They feared it would be a long and cold winter.

CHAPTER 5

A Message from Africa

～

That winter was indeed a cold one. One night in December, all the animals were gathered around the fire. Doctor Dolittle read to them. He translated stories into animal language so they could enjoy them, too. Suddenly Too-Too flew down from the rafters.

"Shh!" the owl said. "What's that noise outside?"

They all listened. Too-Too was right: There was a strange noise coming from outside. It was the sound of something running. Then the door flew open and Chee-Chee ran inside. He was out of breath.

"Doctor!" he cried. "I've just had a message from my cousin in Africa. There is a terrible sickness among the monkeys there. They have all heard of you. They are begging you to come and help."

"Who brought this news?" the doctor asked. He was amazed that a message could arrive from so far away.

"A swallow," Chee-Chee said. "She is still outside near the garden gate."

"Well, bring her in," Doctor Dolittle exclaimed. "It is far too cold outdoors for a little bird, especially a bird from Africa. She can warm herself by the fire."

So the swallow came inside. She was cold and nervous at first. She quickly warmed up by the fire, though. She told them all about the monkey sickness in Africa. It was very serious. They needed Doctor Dolittle right away.

"Of course, of course," the doctor said. "I will leave as soon as possible. I'm worried that we won't have enough money for the tickets, though. Chee-Chee! Would you please hand me the money box?"

The monkey climbed up and took the box from the top shelf of the bookcase. There was nothing in it—not a single penny!

"Nothing!" the doctor exclaimed. "I was certain we had at least a little left."

"Don't you remember that you had to buy Jip a new collar?" Too-Too asked.

"Oh, right," Doctor Dolittle replied. "I forgot about that. Well, I suppose I'll have to go down to the seaside and ask to borrow a boat. Hopefully, one of the fishermen will be kind enough to lend us one."

So the next morning, Doctor Dolittle made his way down to the seaside. He found a fisherman who agreed to lend him a boat to take to Africa. The fisherman knew that Dolittle would not be able to pay him.

"That's all right, Doctor," he said. "You helped my boy a long time ago. And I know how you take care of all those animals. I am glad I can finally help you."

Doctor Dolittle promised to bring the boat back as soon as possible. He then hurried back to his home to tell the animals the good news.

All the animals were very happy! The crocodile, Chee-Chee, and Polynesia were excited to go to Africa. After all, it was where they were born. They had not been back in many years.

"I shall only be able to take you three," Doctor Dolittle said. "And Jip, Dab-Dab, and Gub-Gub, of course. Everyone else will have to stay here. Africa would not be a good place for many of them anyway."

Thankfully, Polynesia had been on many sea

voyages. She told the doctor everything he would need for the trip.

"We will need to bring special food with us," she said. "There is bread called hardtack. It lasts for a long time. We will also need to bring many cans of beans and vegetables. There is always a worry that food will spoil on long trips."

"Yes, yes, of course," the doctor said. He wrote down everything Polynesia told him in his little notebook. "I assume the boat will come with its own anchor."

"Yes, it will have its own anchor," Polynesia said. "But we should make sure we have a lot of rope. Rope is very handy on long sea voyages."

There was still the problem of money. How would they buy everything they needed for their trip if the money box was empty?

You can only imagine Doctor Dolittle's surprise when the butcher arrived at his door with all the supplies!

"I knew that you would need these things for your trip," the butcher said. "Please don't worry about paying me back right now. The grocer and I talked it over. You are doing important work. We'll deal with the bill when you return from Africa."

Doctor Dolittle shook his friend's hand. "My word!" he exclaimed. "You are very good to us. How will I ever thank you?"

"There is no need," the butcher replied. "I am glad to help."

The animals and Doctor Dolittle worked quickly to pack all their things. They turned the water off so the pipes would not freeze while they were away. They put shutters over the windows and gave the key for the stable to the horse. Once they were sure there was enough food and hay for all the animals left behind, they headed off to the seaside.

The butcher, the fisherman, and the grocer were there to see them off. They helped Doctor Dolittle and the animals put their supplies on the boat.

Just as they were about to set sail, Doctor Dolittle realized that he did not know the way to Africa. He asked the fisherman to draw them a map.

"Don't worry, Doctor," the swallow chirped. "I know the way! You can follow me all the way to Africa."

Doctor Dolittle said good-bye to his kind friends. They pulled anchor and set sail. Their voyage had begun!

CHAPTER 6

The Long Journey

⌒

They traveled over the sea for six weeks.
Although that may seem like a long time, it
was actually a short trip. They did not want to
waste time. They followed the swallow all day
as she flew in front of the boat. At night, she
held a tiny lantern so they would not lose their
way.

As they sailed south, the weather became
warmer. Polynesia, Chee-Chee, and the crocodile
were very happy. They ran about the boat laughing. They looked over the side of the boat hoping

to be the first to see Africa. Soon they would be home!

The pig, dog, and owl were not as happy with the weather. It was much harder for them to be hot. The only thing they could do was sit in the shade with their tongues hanging out and sip lemonade.

Dab-Dab the duck kept herself cool by swimming in the ocean behind the boat. Sometimes she dove underwater and swam beneath the boat. She caught many fish, too. Everyone was happy to have fish for dinner. It was a nice change from canned beans and vegetables.

One day, a group of dolphins swam beside their boat. Polynesia sat on the rail so she could talk to them. The dolphins asked if this was Doctor Dolittle's boat. Polynesia answered yes.

"We're so glad to hear that," the dolphins replied. "The monkeys will be happy. They've been worried."

"We should be there soon," Polynesia said. "The swallow says we will arrive in a few days."

"Would you mind if we swam with you for a while?" the dolphins asked. "It would be an honor to travel with Doctor Dolittle."

Polynesia said, "Yes, of course!" She felt very proud. After all, she was the one who had taught Doctor Dolittle to speak animal languages. Now all the animals had heard of him.

Two days later, as the sun was setting, Doctor Dolittle grabbed the telescope. "Everyone!" he called. "Come look! Our journey is about to end. I can see the shores of Africa!"

All the animals ran to his side. They each took a turn looking through the telescope. Everyone cheered that they were so close.

"How long before we reach land?" Jip the dog asked.

"We should be there by morning, I imagine," Doctor Dolittle said.

Just then the sky turned dark and the wind picked up. Everyone ran into the cabin to keep dry during the storm. There was thunder and lightning. It started to rain. The waves were so high that water poured over the deck.

Everyone went to sleep. They hoped the storm would be over by morning. In the middle of the night there came a loud *bang!* The boat stopped and started to roll over on its side.

"What on earth happened?" the doctor called. He opened the cabin door and climbed back on deck. It was difficult to walk through the wind and rain.

"I think we're shipwrecked," Polynesia said.

"We must have run into Africa," Doctor Dolittle said. "Dear me! I hope we haven't ruined the boat."

"I'll take a look," Dab-Dab said. The duck dove over the side and swam underwater to examine the bottom of the boat. There was a large hole from hitting the rocks. Water was pouring inside, and they were sinking fast. Dab-Dab flew back on deck and gave them the news.

Some of the animals began to panic. It was all right for the crocodile and Jip, since they could swim. Polynesia, the sparrow, the duck, and Too-Too could fly. But Chee-Chee and Gub-Gub could not swim or fly.

"Get the rope!" Polynesia called. "I told you the rope would come in handy. Dab-Dab, we need your help again. Take the end of this rope. Fly over to land and tie one end around a tree."

Dab-Dab did as she was told. The wind was strong, but she did not lose her way. She tied a tight knot around a tree. Doctor Dolittle tied the other end around the rail of the boat.

"Now," Polynesia said, "anyone who can't swim or fly should climb along the rope. That way, we'll all get to shore." And that was exactly how all the animals made it safely to land.

Doctor Dolittle put his trunk and some medical supplies into a basket. He hooked the basket onto the rope and sent it to shore. He followed right after.

The boat was not in good shape, though. The hole in the bottom was too big. The waves were too high. The boat banged against the rocks. It was starting to fall apart, board by board. Doctor Dolittle hated to leave it, but there was nothing he could do. "I'll have to find another way to repay the fisherman," he said.

They all took shelter in a cave until the rain stopped. Even though they were all wet from the storm, the cave was dry and comfortable. When they woke up in the morning, the sun was shining. They went back down to the sandy beach to dry out.

"Oh, good old Africa!" Polynesia said. "You know, I haven't been here in over a hundred years but it looks exactly the same. The same beaches, the same palm trees. Oh, it's wonderful to be home!"

Doctor Dolittle and the other animals noticed there were tears in her eyes. She was that happy to see her home again.

"Oh no!" Doctor Dolittle exclaimed. The animals turned to look at him. They all wondered what was wrong.

"I've lost my hat!" he said. "It must have blown away in the storm. That's such a shame. I rather liked that hat."

Dab-Dab said she would go look for it. She flew back over the ocean. After a few minutes, she saw his high hat floating on the water. She flew down to pick up the hat when she noticed one of the white mice riding inside.

"What are you doing here?" Dab-Dab asked. "The doctor told you to stay back in Puddleby."

"But I have relatives in Africa," the mouse said. "Also, I was curious to go on a sea voyage. So

I hid in some luggage and came along. I was very lucky that the hat and I were blown off the ship at the same time. I grabbed a hold of the hat and have been riding in it ever since."

Dab-Dab picked up the hat with the mouse in it and carried both of them back to shore. Everyone gathered around to have a look.

They all agreed that the mouse could not walk through the jungle on his own. So they tried to find a place in the trunk where he could travel comfortably. Just then, they heard the sound of something walking through the trees. They all stopped to listen.

A man stepped out of the jungle and looked at them. He asked them what they were doing there.

"My name is Doctor Dolittle," the doctor said. "I've been asked to come to Africa to help the monkeys. They are very sick, you know."

"You must speak with the king first," the man said.

"What king?" Doctor Dolittle asked. "I'm afraid we don't have time for that." He wanted to get to the monkeys right away.

"All this land belongs to the king," the man said. "All strangers must be brought before him. Follow me."

Doctor Dolittle realized there was no point in arguing. So they gathered up their baggage and followed the man through the jungle. They stopped when they came to a clearing. It was a wide-open space with a building at one end. This was the king's palace. It was not a large palace. In fact, it was quite small. But it was well made and strong. It kept the rain out when it rained. And was cool inside when it was hot outside. In other words, it was perfect for the king, queen, and prince to live in.

The king and queen sat in front of the palace underneath a large umbrella. The king was reading some important papers, and the queen was sound asleep in her chair. The king looked up as Doctor Dolittle and the animals approached.

"And who are you?" the king asked. He did not sound pleased to have visitors.

"Well, you see," Doctor Dolittle said, "we've come about the monkeys." The doctor then told the story of the cold winter night and the sparrow. He told the king about the kind fisherman who lent them the boat. He also told him about the storm and how the boat crashed against the rocks and sank.

"That is all very interesting," the king said, although he did not sound at all interested. "But you cannot pass through my land. I let another man like you use my land once. I was very nice to him, in fact. Then he left big holes in the ground after digging for gold. He disappeared in the middle of the night without saying thank you. I vowed never to let a visitor take advantage of me again."

"But we mean you no harm," Doctor Dolittle pleaded. "We only want to help the sick monkeys."

The king did not listen. He waved to his bodyguards.

"Take this man and his animals away," he said. "Lock them up in the prison. I want them out of my sight."

So the bodyguards led them all away and locked them up in a stone prison. It was a small room with high walls. There was only one window, and it was very high up. The door was thick and strong.

Everyone's spirits were low. No one had expected anything like this to happen. Poor Gub-Gub started to cry. Chee-Chee became angry and told the pig to stop.

"Now, now," Doctor Dolittle said. "It won't do us any good if we fight among ourselves. We need to think clearly about what to do next."

Only then did Doctor Dolittle notice that Polynesia was not with them. He called for her but there was no reply.

"I don't think I've seen her since we were talking to the king," Doctor Dolittle said. "Oh, I hope she's all right."

"She's probably just gone off," the crocodile grumbled. "That's just like her! She's probably with all her old friends right now. She was so excited about coming back to Africa. That's all she talked about. Now she's left us trapped in here."

"I'm not that kind of bird," Polynesia said as she climbed out of Doctor Dolittle's coat pocket.

"Polynesia!" Doctor Dolittle cried. "I'm so happy to see you."

"You should be," Polynesia said. "I'm small enough to fit through that tiny window up there. I was worried that they'd put me in a cage, so I hid in Doctor Dolittle's coat."

"Goodness me," Doctor Dolittle exclaimed. "You're lucky I didn't sit on you!"

"Now listen," Polynesia said. "I have a plan." She jumped onto a bench so she could see the other animals and the doctor clearly.

"Tonight, as soon as it gets dark, I'll sneak through the window and fly back to the palace. Then I'll find a way to convince the king to let us pass through," she said.

"How will you do that?" Gub-Gub the pig asked. "You're only a bird."

"Quite true," Polynesia said. "But you must remember that I can speak man's language. I'm sure I'll think of something clever."

So that night when the moon was shining, Polynesia flew to the high tiny window. She slipped outside easily. She flew to the palace. One of the kitchen windows was broken. Polynesia climbed in through the hole in the glass.

She moved quietly through the palace until she found the king's bedroom. She opened the door gently and peeked in. The queen was away at a dance, but king was sound asleep and snoring in his bed.

Polynesia moved quickly across the room. She did not fly, because she knew the flap of wings might be too loud. She hid underneath his bed.

Then Polynesia coughed. It sounded exactly like Doctor Dolittle's cough. She could imitate anyone.

The king woke up. "Is that you dear?" he called. He thought it was his wife returning from the dance.

The parrot coughed again.

The king sat up in bed. "Who is that?" he said.

"I am Doctor Dolittle," Polynesia said. She sounded exactly like the doctor, too.

"What are you doing in my bedroom?" the king asked. He looked around the room. He could

not see anyone standing in the dark room. "I had you locked up in the prison! How dare you escape! Where are you? I don't see you."

Polynesia laughed. It was a slow, deep, jolly laugh much like Doctor Dolittle's.

"Stop laughing!" the king shouted. He was getting upset. "Come here at once so I can see you!"

"Foolish king," she said. "Have you forgotten that you are talking to the great Doctor Dolittle?" Polynesia tried to make her voice as loud as possible. "Of course you cannot see me!" she said. "I have made myself invisible. There is nothing I cannot do."

"Why are you here?" the king cried.

"I have come to warn you," Polynesia said. "If you do not set me and my animals free, I will cause a sickness throughout your land. If I can make people well, I can certainly make them sick."

Polynesia was not happy with telling lies. She did not know what else to do, though. Tricking the king was her only option.

"You wouldn't do such a thing," the king exclaimed. "Would you?"

"I'm afraid so," Polynesia said. "You must set us all free then let us pass through your land. Remember, Your Highness, do not try my patience."

The king began to tremble. He jumped from his bed. "Doctor," he cried, "it shall be as you say. I will take care of it right away." He then ran out the door to talk to the guards.

As soon as the king left the bedroom, Polynesia crawled from beneath the bed. She flew quietly back downstairs and left through the kitchen window.

Unfortunately, the queen was coming home at the same time. She saw the parrot sneak out through the window. She thought this was a strange thing. When the king returned to the bedroom, he told her all about his mysterious visitor. The queen immediately knew the truth.

"You are such a fool!" she said. "That was not the doctor! It was his parrot. I saw her leave through the kitchen window. She tricked you!"

The king was furious! He rushed to the prison but it was too late. The guards had already opened the door. Doctor Dolittle and his animals were gone.

CHAPTER 7

The Bridge of Apes

The king was so angry! He could not sleep a wink all night. He stormed around his room, shaking his fists in the air.

"How dare they trick me like that!" he said. "No one treats me like that! I am the king!" He called everyone a fool. He threw his toothbrush at the palace cat.

The queen had never seen her husband so angry. She knew that he felt embarrassed. It was hard to admit that a parrot tricked him.

He sent all his guards into the jungle to catch Doctor Dolittle. Then he sent all the palace staff out—the cooks, the maids, and the housekeepers. Even the queen was sent out in a search party.

In the meantime, Doctor Dolittle and his animal friends were rushing through the jungle. They knew they had to reach the sick monkeys as quickly as possible. They suspected the king would eventually discover the trick and send guards after them. Unfortunately, they did not realize how quickly they had been found out.

Gub-Gub the pig had short legs. He tired out very quickly, so the doctor carried him. This made their travels more difficult. They had to pull the trunk full of medicine with them, too.

The king thought it would be easy to find Doctor Dolittle and friends. He thought they would easily get lost in the jungle. He was wrong, though. Chee-Chee the monkey knew the land.

He helped them rush through the jungle. He knew the shortcuts to the Land of the Monkeys.

Chee-Chee and Polynesia knew all the fruit and vegetables that grew in the jungle. This was very helpful. The group had to travel for several days. The monkey and parrot knew where to find water. They found figs and dates and nuts. They knew how to make a delicious drink from oranges and honey.

At night, they all slept in tents made of palm leaves. They made thick soft beds out of dried grass. It was quite comfortable, and they all slept well.

It was good to rest after so much walking. The doctor made a fire out of sticks and leaves. After supper, they would sit in a circle around the fire singing songs. Sometimes Chee-Chee told a story about the jungle.

The monkey knew many, many stories. Monkeys, you see, have no history books. There is nothing written down to remember all the tales. So they keep their stories alive by telling them over and over. Chee-Chee learned all his stories from his mother and father. They had learned the stories from their own parents. In this way, the stories and history of the monkeys were not lost.

Some of these stories were very, very old. Chee-Chee had tales from the time when man still lived in caves and wore animal skins. This was the time before man knew about fire. He told the animals about the great mammoths that nibbled on treetops and lizards with tails as long as trains. Sometimes Chee-Chee talked for so long that the fire burned down to nothing but ashes. Then they all had to scurry around to find more sticks to build a new one.

After the first night in the jungle, the king's guards and staff returned to the palace. The king was angry that they had returned without the prisoners. "Go back into the jungle," he ordered. "Do not return until you have the doctor!"

So while Doctor Dolittle's party made their way through the jungle, thinking they were out of danger, they were being followed. If Chee-Chee had known this, he would have been more careful to hide them.

One day, Chee-Chee climbed to the top of a tree. He looked out over the land in front of them. He climbed back down excited. "We are close to the Land of the Monkeys," he said. "We should be there very soon."

An hour or two later, they were surprised by a group of monkeys. One of them was Chee-Chee's cousin. The monkeys were sitting in trees near the edge of a swamp waiting for them. When they saw Doctor Dolittle approach, the monkeys started to shout and thump on the trees. They cheered and waved leaves. They jumped up and down.

Several of the monkeys surrounded the trav-elers. They grabbed Doctor Dolittle's bag and trunk. They even helped carry Gub-Gub. Some of the monkeys ran ahead to tell the others that the great Doctor Dolittle had arrived.

The king's men were still following the doc-tor and the animals. They heard the monkeys cheer and knew they were close. They hurried toward the noise. They wanted to catch the group so they could all go home.

The monkey who volunteered to carry Gub-Gub was moving slowly. He was trailing behind the others as they made their way toward the village. He heard a noise behind him, so he turned around. That's when he noticed the captain of the king's guard sneaking through the trees. The monkey walked quickly to catch up with the doctor.

The captain saw the monkey speed up, so he started to run, too. Then all the guards followed him. The men ran fast. They ran harder than they ever had before, with no stopping. They knew they were so close to catching Doctor Dolittle and his friends.

Everyone was running now! Doctor Dolittle, his animals, the monkeys, and the king's guards. The poor doctor was not used to so much activity. He slipped and fell down in the mud. The captain of the guards saw him fall. He was certain he would catch the doctor at last.

It was at that moment that the captain fell down, too. He did not notice that a pair of monkeys was waiting for him. They had placed a stick across the path to trip the captain. As soon as he fell down, the monkeys raced away. This gave Doctor Dolittle time to stand up. He raced along the road after the monkeys.

"Don't worry," Chee-Chee called to everyone behind him. "We're almost there!" However, they had one more obstacle to face. The king's land ended at a steep cliff. There was a river far below. One the other side, on top of another steep cliff, was the Land of the Monkeys.

Jip the dog looked at the Land of the Monkeys across the gap. "Golly!" he said. "How will we get across? The king's guards will be here at any minute."

The big monkey who was carrying Gub-Gub dropped the pig to the ground. "Quick!" he shouted to the other monkeys. "A bridge! We need to make a bridge!"

The doctor looked around him. He wondered what they would use to make the bridge. There were a few pieces of loose wood but not enough for a bridge. He turned to look back into the jungle, wondering if there was something he missed. When he turned back to look over the gap, he saw that the monkeys had already built the bridge. They were using their own bodies! By holding hands and feet, they stretched themselves across the gap from the king's land to the Land of the Monkeys.

They shouted to the doctor that he should start across. "Walk over!" they called. "Hurry! Walk over. All of you."

Doctor Dolittle was the last to cross. Just as he

was getting to the other side, the king's men arrived at the cliff. They shook their fists and yelled with rage. They knew they were too late. The doctor and his animals were safe in the Land of the Monkeys. The monkeys pulled one another across to the other side.

"You should know, Doctor Dolittle," Chee-Chee said, "many explorers and scientists have waited quietly in the bushes hoping to see that bridge. We never let men see that trick. You are the first to see the Bridge of Apes." The doctor said that he felt very pleased.

It would have been nice to relax now that everyone was safe in the Land of the Monkeys. But there was no time. Doctor Dolittle got to work right away helping the sick monkeys.

CHAPTER 8

The Leader of the Lions

⌒

Doctor Dolittle's first job was to separate the sick animals from the healthy ones. He then asked Chee-Chee and his cousin to build a grass hut. He brought all the healthy monkeys to the hut and gave them a needle full of medicine in the arm. At first the monkeys were scared of the needle, but they understood it would prevent them from getting the monkey sickness. They arrived from all the hills and valleys surrounding the Land of the Monkeys. It took three days and three nights to give needles to all the monkeys.

Chee-Chee and his cousin also built another house. This one had a lot of beds in it. Doctor Dolittle put all the sick monkeys in this building.

But there were too many sick monkeys and not enough well monkeys to nurse them. So Doctor Dolittle sent word out into the jungle. He asked other animals to come help. Leopards, antelopes, and giraffe all arrived to pitch in.

The lions, however, were a different story. The leader of the lions was very proud. He arrived at the house of sick monkeys to speak with Doctor Dolittle.

"Do you really expect me to help the monkeys?" he asked. "I am the king of the lions. I am the king of all the beasts! I don't have time to waste on sick monkeys!"

The lion's voice was quite frightening. Doctor Dolittle did his best to not sound scared. "Now, listen to me. The day may come when the lions are sick. If you don't help the monkeys now, you might find the lions all alone when they need help."

"The lions are never in trouble," the lion roared. "The lions only make trouble." He walked back into the jungle thinking he was rather smart and clever.

When the leopards heard about the lions, they left, too. Then the antelopes said they knew nothing about nursing monkeys. They were too shy to speak like the lion. They pawed the ground and did not look Doctor Dolittle in the eye as they spoke.

Doctor Dolittle became very worried. Without the animals' help, how could he tend to all the sick monkeys?

When the king of lion returned home, his wife ran out to meet him. She was very upset.

"One of the cubs won't eat," she cried. "I don't know what to do! He hasn't eaten anything since last night." She began to cry.

The king of the lions went in to look at his cubs. One boy ran up to meet his father. He was his usual happy and excited self. The other little cub did not look well. He lay in his bed and could only smile weakly at his father. The lion kissed both his cubs on the tops of their heads.

His wife was waiting for him outside. He told her about meeting Doctor Dolittle. "He wanted us to care for the sick monkeys. The monkeys! I told him that a lion would never do such a thing."

"Excuse me?" his wife said. She was angry. "Why would you say that?"

The king of the lions was shocked by his wife's reaction. He sat quietly listening.

"All the animals are talking about this wonderful man," she continued. "They say he can cure any kind of illness and he's very nice. He's the only man in the world who can speak animal language. And now, when we have a sick baby, you say something to offend him!"

"But, but, dear," the lion stammered.

"Go back to the doctor right now!" she cried. "Tell him that you're sorry. Take all the lions and all the other animals with you. Do whatever the doctor asks you to do. If we're lucky, he'll come to look at our sick cub later."

So the lion went back to the doctor. He said, "I happened to be passing this way and thought I'd look in. Have you found any help yet?"

"No," Doctor Dolittle said. "I haven't, and I'm very worried."

"That's too bad," the lion said. He tried not to look sheepish. "Well, since you're having so much trouble, I suppose I could help in some way."

"Thank you!" Doctor Dolittle said. "That's so kind of you."

"I told the leopards to come back. The antelopes will also do their share," the lion added.

"That is indeed kind of you," the doctor said. "We'll get to work right away!"

"Oh," the lion said. "One more thing. We have a sick cub at our place. I'm sure it's nothing, but my wife is worried. Maybe you could stop by when you're done here."

"Of course, of course," Doctor Dolittle said. "I'll go as soon as I can." He was very happy. At last, curing the monkeys seemed possible.

All the jungle animals returned to help. In fact, there were so many animals that he had to turn some away. After the first week, half of the sick monkeys were better. By the end of the second week, they were all cured.

Doctor Dolittle's work was done. He was so tired he went to bed and slept for three days without even turning over.

CHAPTER 9

The Monkeys' Council

⌒

The first thing Doctor Dolittle did when he awoke was to announce he must go home. "It's time to return to Puddleby," he said. "I've been away long enough."

All the jungle animals were surprised to hear this. They all thought he would stay with them forever. So that night, all the monkeys got together to talk it over.

The chief chimpanzee stood up first. "Why would he go away? Is he not happy with us?"

Then the Grand Gorilla stood up. "I think we

should ask him to stay. Perhaps if we build him a bigger house and a comfortable bed, he won't want to leave."

Now Chee-Chee got up. All the others whispered, "Shh! Chee-Chee is going to speak."

"My friends," Chee-Chee said, "I am afraid it is useless to ask the doctor to stay. He has many responsibilities back home in Puddleby. There are other animals waiting for him. The horse will be quite worried by now. There are friends he left behind. Also, a fisherman was kind enough to lend him a boat. That boat crashed against the rocks, so Doctor Dolittle will have to replace it. It wouldn't be fair if he stayed here."

The monkeys were silent for some time. They sat on the ground thinking carefully. At long last, one of the baboons stood up.

"I don't think we should let this good man leave without giving him something. We should think of a present wonderful enough to say thank you for all his work. He needs to know how grateful we all are."

A tiny red monkey at the back of the group stood up. "I agree! We need to find the perfect gift."

"We should give him a giant bag of coconuts!" one monkey yelled.

"A hundred bunches of bananas!" said another.

Chee-Chee shook his head. "Those are wonderful ideas but they would be too heavy to carry home. Also, they would probably go bad before they were half eaten."

"I know!" said the little red monkey. "I know exactly what we should give him. A pushmi-pullyu."

"That's a wonderful idea," Chee-Chee said. "No one back home has ever seen a pushmi-pullyu. That's perfect!"

CHAPTER 10

The Rarest Animal of All

∽

The pushmi-pullyus are now extinct. There are no more to be found anywhere on earth. In the days when Doctor Dolittle lived, there were still a few in the jungles of Africa. Even then, though, they were very, very rare.

They had no tail but a head at each end. There were sharp horns on each head. They were shy and terribly hard to catch. You could not sneak up on pushmi-pullyus, as they could always see you coming. Also, their heads slept at different times. So no pushmi-pullyu had ever been caught.

Many hunters had tried over the years, but none was successful.

So the monkeys set out to find a pushmi-pullyu. It was several miles into the jungle when one of them spotted unusual hoof prints. These were fresh tracks. They knew that a pushmi-pullyu was close by.

They walked along the riverbank, following the tracks. They noticed a place where the grass was thick and tall. It was the perfect hiding place for a pushmi-pullyu.

They all joined hands and made a giant circle around the grassy spot. The pushmi-pullyu heard them and tried to run away. He could not break through the ring of monkeys, though. When he saw that there was no use trying to escape, he sat down. He waited to see what would happen next.

"We would like to ask a favor," the Grand Gorilla said. "Would you go back to Puddleby with Doctor Dolittle? We are grateful for all he's done. We want to give him something very special."

"Oh, most certainly not," the pushmi-pullyu said. "I could never do that!"

The monkeys explained to him that he would not be put into a zoo. He would live with the doctor at his home and have a wonderful life.

The pushmi-pullyu shook his head. "No. You know how shy I am. I would hate to be stared at."

The monkeys tried to convince him that he would enjoy living with the good doctor.

After quite some time, the pushmi-pullyu agreed to meet with Doctor Dolittle. If he liked him, he would consider going with him.

So the pushmi-pullyu and the monkeys traveled back to Doctor Dolittle's grass hut. They knocked on the door. The duck was packing the trunk. She turned to the door and said, "Come in!"

Chee-Chee brought the pushmi-pullyu inside. He was very proud.

"My goodness!" the doctor exclaimed. "What on earth is that?" He couldn't believe his eyes.

"My word!" Dab-Dab the duck said. She looked at the strange animal with a head on both ends of its body. "How does it make up its mind?"

"This is the pushmi-pullyu," said Chee-Chee. "It is the rarest animal in all the African jungles. It is the only two-headed beast in the world. If you take him home with you, all your money troubles will be solved. People will pay any money to see him."

"But I don't want any money," said the doctor.

"Yes, you do," said Dab-Dab. "You always forget that we need money to live."

"Don't you remember how we had to scrimp and save?" asked Jip. "Also, we borrowed the fisherman's boat and now it's ruined. How will we pay him back if we don't have any money?"

"I was going to build him one," said the doctor sheepishly.

"Oh, do be sensible!" cried Dab-Dab. "You're not a carpenter. You've never built anything out of wood. You would have no idea where to start. Chee-Chee is right. We need to take this funny-looking creature with us."

"Well, I do see your point," murmured the doctor. "I don't think that would be a very nice move for him, though. I would hate for him to leave this lovely place to go on display. It wouldn't seem fair. But would he—I'm sorry, I forgot his name—would he like to come home with us?"

"Yes, I'll go," said the pushmi-pullyu. He had seen at once that Doctor Dolittle was a man to be trusted. "You have been so kind to all the animals here. The monkeys tell me that I am the only one who will do. But you must promise me one thing."

"Of course," Doctor Dolittle said. "Whatever you would like."

"If I don't like living in your land, you must promise to send me back."

"Why, certainly," he said. "Excuse me, would you mind if I asked you a question?"

"Please go ahead," the pushmi-pullyu said.

Doctor Dolittle took his book out of his pocket and started to make notes. "I notice that you only speak with one mouth. Can you talk with the other one?"

"Certainly," the pushmi-pullyu said. "I just like to save the other one for eating. That way, I can talk while I eat and not appear rude."

When the packing was done and they were ready to go, the monkeys threw a party for their friends. All the animals of the jungle came. They ate pineapples and mangoes and honey. There were all sorts of good things to eat and drink.

The doctor stood up to make a speech.

"My friends," he said. "I have never been very good at speeches but I'll try. I want to tell you all how sad I am to leave this beautiful land. I wish I could stay, but I have too many responsibilities in my own home. Although I came here for sad reasons, I'm glad that I was able to come and help."

All the animals cheered and saluted the good doctor.

"Please remember that you should never let flies settle on your food before you eat it. And do not sleep on the ground when the rains are coming." Doctor Dolittle paused for a moment. "And I hope—I hope you will all live happily ever after."

The Grand Gorilla rolled up a large rock. He placed it near the door of the hut. "This rock will mark the spot where Doctor Dolittle once lived. The great doctor who traveled so far to save the monkeys of the African jungle."

The animals cheered again, and a tear came to the doctor's eye. It was a wonderful tribute. And even today, if you go to that spot in the jungle, you will see the rock.

Then, when the party was over, the doctor and his animals started on their way to the seashore. All the monkeys went with him as far as the edge of their country, carrying the trunk and bags, to see them off.

CHAPTER 11

The Prince's Story

◦

They stopped and said farewell by the edge of the river. This took a very long time, as all the monkeys wanted to shake Doctor Dolittle's hand.

Afterward, as the doctor and his animals walked alone, Polynesia said, "We must be careful. We are walking through the king's land again. I'm sure he's still angry with us. That was an awful trick I played on him."

"Yes, but the thing that has me worried," Doctor Dolittle said, "is how we will get another boat to get home. I don't know if we'll be lucky enough to find someone as kind as our fisherman friend back home."

The walk back took many days. One day, while they were passing through a thick part of the jungle, Chee-Chee went ahead of them looking for coconuts. Unfortunately, while he was away, the doctor and other animals got lost. They wandered around and around but could not find their way down to the seashore.

Chee-Chee was upset when he realized that his friends were lost. He climbed high into the trees for a better view. He looked for Doctor Dolittle's high hat, but it was nowhere to be seen. He shouted. He waved. He clapped his hands. It was no use. They seemed to have disappeared altogether.

Indeed, they had lost their way. They strayed far off the path. The jungle was so thick with bushes and vines that it was difficult to move at all. The doctor used his pocketknife to cut his way through the branches. They stumbled into wet, boggy places. They scratched themselves on thorns. There seemed to be no end of trouble, yet they could not find their way back to the path.

At last, after hours of wandering through the jungle, they stumbled into the king's back garden by accident. The king's men rushed to them immediately and captured them.

Polynesia, always a quick thinker, flew off into the treetops before they saw her. The doctor and the rest were taken to the king.

"Aha!" the king said when he saw them. "So you are caught again. This time you will not escape. This doctor who thinks he's so clever will be scrubbing my kitchen floors for the rest of his life. Guards! Take them to the prison."

So the doctor and his animals were led back to the small dungeon. They were all very upset.

"This is such a shame," Doctor Dolittle said. "I really must get back to Puddleby. The fisherman will think that I've stolen his boat. And the animals will need tending by now."

All this time, Polynesia was sitting in a tall tree near the garden. She looked into the distance and saw Chee-Chee swinging in the trees. He was still looking for them. When he saw her, he moved quickly to her side. He asked what had happened to everyone else.

"The doctor and all the animals have been captured by the king's men," she whispered. "We lost our way in the jungle. We ended up in the back garden by accident."

"Couldn't you guide them?" Chee-Chee asked. "You know your way through the jungle." He began to scold her for not taking care of them while he looked for coconuts.

"It was all the pig's fault," said Polynesia. "He kept running off looking for roots and other treats. I had to keep going to look for him. Then I forgot where I had turned left or where I had turned right."

"Careful!" Chee-Chee said. He held a finger to his lips. "Look, it's the prince wandering through the garden. We have to be careful that he doesn't notice us."

The prince did not look happy. He sat down beneath a tree and hung his head. He was holding a book. He opened it up but did not start reading. He leafed through the pages and sighed.

"If only I could live in these stories," the prince said out loud. "I am a prince and I live in a palace but it is not like the fairy tales. Our palace is not as grand. I do not have as many beautiful things. I wish I looked like the heroes in these stories. I wish that was my life!"

The prince closed his eyes and held the book to his chest. He sighed once more.

Chee-Chee suddenly had an idea. He whispered

it to Polynesia. She nodded, then flew down to a branch closer to the prince.

"Young prince!" she said. She spoke softly in a high, gentle voice. She did not want to scare him. She wanted him to hear a friendly voice instead. "Young prince!" she said again.

The prince opened his eyes. He looked all around him but could not see anyone. He did not think of looking in the trees! He did not suspect it was a parrot talking to him.

"Yes?" he said. "Who's there?"

"It doesn't matter who I am," she said. "I have come to tell you something very important."

"I don't understand," he said. Despite Polynesia's best efforts, the prince was nervous.

"I am the queen of the fairies," Polynesia said. "I have heard your wishes."

"Really?" the prince said. He had read stories about the queen of the fairies but did not know she actually existed.

"Yes," she said. "I can hear the wishes of everyone in the jungle. Unfortunately, I don't have time to help everyone. I can only pick special people and special wishes."

"And you are here to answer my wish?" the prince asked. He sat up straight. This was very exciting news!

"I understand that you want to look and act like the heroes in fairy tales," Polynesia said.

"Yes! Yes, please!" the prince exclaimed. He was excited. He had been so sad a moment ago. Now he was going to be a hero in a fairy tale!

"Although I am queen of the fairies," Polynesia continued, "I'm not able to help you all on my own."

"What do I need to do?" the prince asked.

"You need to see Doctor Dolittle," she said. "He is the smartest man in all the world! He will make you dreams come true."

"Doctor Dolittle?" he replied. "But how will I

find him? I'm only a young prince, and I live so far away from everyone."

"You are a lucky prince," Polynesia said. "It just so happens that Doctor Dolittle is here right now! He is sitting in your father's prison. He knows everything about magic and medicine. He is the only one who can help you."

"But what can I do?" the prince said.

"You must go to see the doctor, of course," Polynesia said. "But do it in secret. Wait until the sun has gone down. Then sneak over to the prison and talk to him. He will know exactly how to help you. And now, I must leave. I must get back to Fairy Land."

"Thank you, queen of the fairies!" the prince said. He waved his hand and smiled, even though he did not know which way to face.

Then he leaned his head back and smiled. The prince sat quietly beneath the tree. He waited for the sun to set.

CHAPTER 12

Medicine and Magic

൙

Polynesia moved quietly. She slipped out of the tree and flew to the prison. Once again, she entered the cell through the high window.

All the animals were sitting quietly on the floor. They looked worried. It was scary being back in the prison.

Doctor Dolittle, however, was taking a nap. Polynesia cleared her throat until the doctor woke up. He sat up and rubbed the sleep from his eyes.

"Listen," Polynesia said. "Chee-Chee and I have a plan. The prince is going to come see you tonight. I told him that you have magical powers. He wants you to turn him into a fairy tale hero."

"Excuse me?" Doctor Dolittle cried. "How on earth will I do that? I'm a doctor. I know nothing about magic."

"Doctor Dolittle is right," Dab-Dab said. "You can't just turn the prince into someone from a book. That's impossible."

"Well," Polynesia continued. "I convinced the prince that it was true. I've already done my part. Now you need to do yours. Then when he offers a reward, you must ask to be set free."

Doctor Dolittle sighed. "Very well," he said. "When will the prince be here?"

"He is coming to see you after the sun sets," Polynesia replied.

"Then I suppose I should get to work," he said. He took his notebook out of his pocket. "I have only a few hours to think of a plan."

That night the prince visited the prison. He told the guards to wait by the door and stepped inside the cell. He felt nervous talking to the great doctor but tried to sound strong.

"Good evening, Doctor," he said. "The queen of the fairies said I should speak to you. She said you could help me."

"Of course," Doctor Dolittle said. "I'll do whatever I can." The doctor sounded as kind and helpful as always. He could not even pretend to be mean.

"I love to read," the prince said. "I read all the time. It is my favorite thing to do. But there is never anyone in the stories like me. They wear fancy clothes. They all have blond hair and blue eyes. They all have horses and fight dragons."

"I see," Doctor Dolittle said. "You would like to be like the people in the stories."

"Yes! Exactly," the prince said.

"You do know that it's very hard to be happy when you try to be someone that you're not," Doctor Dolittle said.

"I know what I want," the prince said. "I want to be like a hero in a fairy tale!"

"Very well, then," the doctor said. "You will have to excuse me a moment. I need to mix together some medicine. We'll need a special potion."

Doctor Dolittle turned to his medicine bag. He took out different bottles. He poured some into a bowl and mixed them up. This was not real medicine. Polynesia had spent the afternoon gathering water for him. When he was finished mixing, he turned back to the prince.

"You must drink this quickly," he said. "Try to drink it all in three gulps."

The prince took the bowl and did exactly as Doctor Dolittle asked.

"How are you feeling?" Doctor Dolittle asked.

"I don't know," the prince stuttered. "I don't really know if I feel anything . . ."

Just then, Jip started to bark. He stood in front of the prince and barked up at him.

The prince stepped back. "What is wrong with your dog?"

Then Dab-Dab started to quack. Too-Too hooted at the prince.

"Goodness me!" Doctor Dolittle exclaimed. "The potion is working quickly!"

"Really?" the prince said. "Do you have a mirror?

"No, I'm sorry," Doctor Dolittle said. "We don't have a mirror."

"But how will I know what has happened? I need to see for myself."

"Well, look at all the animals! They seem very upset. Something incredible must be happening. Everyone knows that animals don't lie."

The prince looked at all the animals. They were certainly very excited. He looked back at the doctor. "Could you describe me, then?"

"Of course," Doctor Dolittle said. "You are much taller. You look just like someone who could fight a dragon."

"But what do I look like?" the prince said. "Am I blond with blue eyes?"

"You look like a hero in the fairy tales," the doctor said.

"Then I must be tall and blond," the prince insisted.

"There are many different kinds of heroes," Doctor Dolittle said.

The prince was very happy. He was certain he was exactly as he imagined. "How can I thank you?" he said.

"You could let us go free," the doctor said. "It is not good for my animals to be locked up like this."

"Of course," the prince said. "I'll tell the guards to let you go right away."

Too-Too cleared his throat. Jip nudged the doctor's leg to remind him. "Oh yes," the doctor said. "We'll also need a boat. We need to get home as soon as possible."

"I can do that as well," the prince said. He moved toward the door.

"Wait!" Doctor Dolittle said. "There's one more important thing. You must stay indoors for at least three hours. No moonlight or wind should touch you. Otherwise the spell won't work."

"Oh, thank you," the prince said. "I'm glad you warned me."

The prince went to the door and opened it just a crack. He stood back so no moonlight would fall on him. The guards could not see him from behind the door.

"Guards!" he called. "I give permission to set these prisoners free. You must escort them to the sea. They will be taking one of our boats. Please make sure that they leave safely."

"But, the king," one of the guards said. "He won't be happy if they are gone."

"I'll worry about my father," the prince said. "Now do as I say and take them to the water."

The guards did as they were told. Doctor Dolittle and the animals followed them to the sea. The guards pointed to a boat.

"You can take that one," a guard said. "We have to get back to the prison now. We don't have time to help you on board."

"That's all right," Doctor Dolittle said. "We thank you for bringing us here."

Once the guards had left, all the animals sighed.

"That was a good plan," Gub-Gub said. "The prince really believed that Jip was upset."

"How did you think to trick him like that?" Too-Too asked. "How did you know he would believe you?"

"He wanted to believe it was true. I knew we only had to pretend and he would believe us."

"It was very clever of you," Polynesia said. "I rather wish that I had thought of it."

"Well, as any good doctor knows," Doctor Dolittle said, "sometimes common sense is the best medicine."

Before Doctor Dolittle and the animals went on the boat, they had to say good-bye. Chee-Chee, Polynesia, and the crocodile had decided to stay in Africa. They loved living with the doctor in Puddleby, but they missed their families too much. It would be too hard to leave them again. It was a sad time for everyone.

Doctor Dolittle, Jip, Gub-Gub, Dab-Dab, the white mouse, the pushmi-pullyu, and Too-Too the owl went on the boat. They looked back to the shore and waved to their friends.

There was a flutter in the trees. Everyone looked toward the jungle. There was a full moon that night, so they could see clearly. Suddenly thousands of swallows flew into the sky.

"I had no idea that we had been in Africa so long," said Doctor Dolittle. "It will be nearly summer when we get home. These must be the swallows who are going back. How kind of you to wait for us," he called to the birds. "We are heading north now. It would help to have you lead us."

So the boat set sail. Doctor Dolittle and his animals stood at the railing. They waved to the friends on shore. Chee-Chee, Polynesia, and the crocodile called good-bye until their throats were sore. The doctor had promised that he would spend his vacations back in Africa with his friends, but it was still a sad moment and they all cried bitter tears.

CHAPTER 13

Red Sails and Blue Wings

✺

On their way home, Doctor Dolittle and his friends had to sail pass the coast of Barbary, home to the Barbary pirates.

These pirates were very bad men. They waited for sailors to shipwreck on the shore. If that did not happen, the pirates got into their own boat and chased them. When they caught ships, they stole everything and sent the passengers off in rowboats.

The pirates were always pleased with themselves. They went back to shore singing songs and thinking themselves very clever.

One sunny day, the doctor and Dab-Dab were exercising on deck. They walked up and down the ship. A nice fresh wind was blowing, and everyone was happy. Dab-Dab was the first to notice the other ship. It was a long way behind them and had a bright red sail.

"I don't like the look of that sail," said Dab-Dab. "I don't think it's friendly. I'm worried more trouble is coming our way."

Jip was sleeping beside them on the deck. He began to growl and talk in his sleep. "I smell roast beef cooking," he mumbled. "Oh, roast beef with brown gravy."

"My goodness!" Doctor Dolittle said. "What's the matter with that dog? Does he smell in his sleep? Smelling and talking?"

"It appears that way," said Dab-Dab. "All dogs can smell in their sleep."

"But he must be imagining it," the doctor said. "There's no roast beef cooking on this boat."

"It must be coming from that other ship."

"But that ship is ten miles away at least," Doctor Dolittle said. "Surely he can't smell that far!"

Jip began to growl again. His lips curled up at the edges. Even though he was still asleep, he began to talk more. "I smell bad men," he mumbled. "The worst men I ever smelled. I smell trouble. Woof! I need to stop them. *Woof!*" Jip started to bark so loud that he woke himself up.

"Look!" Dab-Dab said. "That ship is much closer now! It must be traveling fast. They're coming right at us. I wonder who they are."

"I was just dreaming about them," Jip said. "I could smell them. They are very bad men. My guess is that they are the pirates of Barbary."

"Then we must hurry on our way," the doctor said. "We need to put up more sails to catch the wind. That will help us go faster."

The dog hurried downstairs to grab more

sails. He dragged up as many as he could carry. But even with all these sails, the pirate ship was still faster. It continued to gain on the doctor's ship.

"The prince gave us a poor ship," grumbled Gub-Gub. "It must have been the slowest in his fleet. Look! They are almost on top of us now."

"I can see six men," Jip said. "What are we going to do?"

The doctor asked Dab-Dab to fly up and tell the swallows they were being followed. "Tell them that the pirates' ship is very fast," he added.

When the swallows heard this, they all came down to the deck. They told the doctor to un-ravel some pieces of long rope. They needed to have as many thin strips of rope as possible. They tied the end of these strips to the front of the ship. The swallows took hold of the other ends. They flew back into the sky, pulling the boat behind them.

Swallows, as you may know, are small birds and not very strong. But it is quite different when there are many of them. There were a thousand strings attached to Doctor Dolittle's ship. And there were two swallows pulling on each string.

In only a moment or two the doctor found himself moving so fast that he had to hold on to his hat with both hands. It felt almost like they were flying, too.

All the animals on board began to laugh and dance. They looked back at the pirate ship. It was growing smaller and smaller. The red sail was being left far, far behind.

CHAPTER 14

The Rat's Warning

༼

Dragging a ship through the sea is hard work. So after two or three hours, the swallows began to get tired. Their wings were sore, and they were out of breath. They sent a message down to Doctor Dolittle that they needed to rest. They said they would pull the boat to a nearby island. They could hide it in a bay while they rested.

When they were safely in the bay, Doctor Dolittle told the animals that they could go on land. He knew that they would want to stretch their legs. "I'll go look for some water," he said.

As they were leaving the ship, Doctor Dolittle noticed hundreds of rats coming up from downstairs. They were leaving the ship as well.

A large black rat crept over to the doctor. He coughed a few times, paused to clean his whiskers, and then he spoke.

"Excuse me. You must know, Doctor, that all ships have rats on them," he said shyly.

"Yes," the doctor said. "I've heard that before."

"You must have also heard that rats leave a sinking ship," the rat added.

"Yes," the doctor said. "I've heard that, too."

"I just wanted you to know that we are leaving this ship. But first I wanted to tell you," the rat said, "that this is not a safe ship. The sides aren't strong enough. Its boards are rotten. This ship will not last another day."

"But how do you know?" asked the doctor.

"We always know," answered the rat. "We get a tingly feeling in the ends of our tails. The same feeling you get when your foot falls asleep. And we all got the feeling this morning. At first I thought it was my arthritis coming back. I told my brother and he said he felt the same. Anyway, we all agreed that the problem was the ship. You shouldn't sail on it anymore. Now I must be going. We must look for a good place to live on the island. Good-bye!"

Doctor Dolittle waved to the rat as he ran off the ship. "Thank you for telling us," he called.

So the doctor and his animals left the boat. They carried pots to fill with water. They walked quickly along the beach so as not to disturb the resting swallows.

"I wonder what this island is called," the doctor wondered. "There are certainly a lot of birds here."

"These are the Canary Islands," Dab-Dab said. "Don't you hear the canaries singing?"

"Why, yes!" the doctor cried. "How silly of

me! I wonder if they can tell us where to find water."

So Doctor Dolittle called to the canaries. They were happy to help. They had heard all about Doctor Dolittle from other birds. They showed him around the island, taking him and the animals to waterfalls and green fields. They took them to a fresh spring where they filled their buckets with water. Everyone was quite happy.

The pushmi-pullyu liked the green grass much more than the dried apples he had been eating on the boat. Gub-Gub could dig in the ground for tasty roots. They all liked the valley of wild sugarcane they found near the fresh spring.

Suddenly two swallows flew over to them. They were excited.

"Doctor!" they said. "The pirates have arrived in the bay. They are all on your boat right now."

"All the pirates are on our boat?" Doctor Dolittle asked.

"Yes," the swallows said. "They are stealing everything! We saw them all go downstairs."

"If they are all on our boat," Dab-Dab said, "that means their boat is empty!"

"You have a good point," said Doctor Dolittle. "That's a splendid idea!"

"Idea?" Gub-Gub said. "I didn't hear anyone mention an idea. What are you talking about?"

"I'm sorry, Gub-Gub," Doctor Dolittle said. "There's no time to explain everything. We must hurry!"

He called all the animals together. They said a quick good-bye to the canaries then ran down the beach.

They saw the pirate ship with its red sail standing in the water. Just as the swallows had told them, there was no one on board. So Doctor Dolittle told his animals to walk softly. They all crept to the pirate ship.

CHAPTER 15

The Barbary Dragon

❦

Everything would have been fine if the pig had not caught a cold.

They had pulled the anchor up in perfect silence. The ship started to move quietly out of the bay. Then, just as they were almost away, Gub-Gub sneezed. He sneezed so loudly that the pirates on the other ship rushed back upstairs.

They looked back at their ship and saw it moving out to sea. The pirates pulled anchor and started after the doctor. They were expert sailors.

In only a matter of moments they had moved the boat to the mouth of the bay. They were blocking Doctor Dolittle. He had no way to get back to the open sea.

The pirate leader shook his fist at the doctor. "Aha! You are mine now!" he said. "You thought you could take off in my ship, did you? You are not a good enough sailor to escape me. That is why they call me the Barbary Dragon! No one is stronger than me."

The pirate leader looked at all the animals with Doctor Dolittle. "I want that duck! And the pig! We will have a fine supper tonight." All the other pirates laughed.

Poor Gub-Gub started to cry. Dab-Dab started to think about an escape plan. Too-Too the owl leaned in to whisper in Doctor Dolittle's ear.

"Keep him talking," he said. "Try to be nice so he doesn't become angry. If the rats were correct, our ship will sink very soon. And rats are never wrong. So be calm and keep him talking until the ship sinks."

"But the rats said it would sink by tomorrow morning," Doctor Dolittle whispered. "You expect me to keep him talking until then? Well, I suppose we don't have much choice, do we? I wonder what I should talk about . . ."

When Doctor Dolittle looked back at the pirates, he saw that their boat was closer still. The pirates were laughing. "I wonder which of us will catch the pig!" one of them yelled. They laughed some more.

Poor Gub-Gub was scared. The pushmi-pullyu prepared for a fight. Although they were shy and quiet creatures, pushmi-pullyus defend their friends. And Jip stood between the pig and the pirates, ready to protect Gub-Gub if necessary.

Then the pirates stopped laughing. They

became very serious. Something was upsetting
them. They looked around them puzzled. Something was making them uneasy.

"Thunder and lightning!" the Barbary Dragon
called. "Men, the boat's leaking!"

The pirates looked over the side. They were
sinking! The boat was going lower and lower into
the water.

The front end went down first. It sank so low
that the back end stuck straight up in the air. The
pirates had to hold on to the rails. The sea rushed
and roared in through all the windows and doors.
At last the ship plunged right down to the bottom of the sea. The six bad men were left bobbing
in the water.

Some of them started to swim to shore.
Others tried to get aboard the ship with Doctor
Dolittle. Jip kept close guard by the rails, though.
He nipped and barked as any of them tried to
climb up. The pirates started to panic.

Then one of them noticed something swimming near them in the water. "Sharks!" one of them yelled. "Please. Let us aboard. The sharks will eat us!"

Doctor Dolittle looked in the water by the pirates. He saw the large gray fish swimming in the deep. He had to agree that this looked like a very bad situation.

One of the sharks popped his head out of the water. "Are you Doctor Dolittle?"

"Yes," the doctor said. "You've heard of me?"

"There's no creature on land or in water who hasn't heard of you," the shark said. "Are these men bothering you? We know all about these pirates, too. If you like, we could eat them for you."

"Oh, well," Doctor Dolittle said, "that's kind of you to offer, but I don't think it's necessary. You could do us another favor, though. Would you mind keeping all the pirates in the bay until we leave? It would help if they couldn't reach ship or shore. When we are gone, you could let them go."

"Your wish is our command, Doctor," the shark said. The sharks made a tight circle around the pirates in the water.

The boat was about to set sail when Doctor Dolittle put up his hand. "Wait!" he called. He walked back to the railing and called to the pirates.

"I have one more thing to say," he said. "You must stop being pirates from now on!"

"Excuse me?" the pirate leader said. "Why should we stop being pirates?"

The other pirates laughed. They planned to find another boat as soon as Doctor Dolittle was gone. They would be back to stealing things in no time!

"You will stop being pirates because I said so," Doctor Dolittle replied. "You can see that the sharks listen to me. Well, all the animals on land and sea will listen, too. If you continue to steal things and hurt people, these sharks will not be so kind. You will have trouble with birds, horses, dogs, and monkeys."

The pirate leader looked at the sharks in the water. He knew that the doctor was telling the truth. The animals would never leave them alone.

"But what will we do?" he asked. "We don't know how to be anything else."

"You could learn to be farmers," Doctor Dolittle said. "That is a good honest job. You could help people rather than steal from them."

The pirate leader was about to complain when he felt a shark brush against his foot.

"Okay! Okay!" he called. "We'll be farmers. We promise. Can we go to shore now?"

"Yes, that's fine," the doctor said. He told the sharks to let them swim to shore.

"But Doctor Dolittle," Dab-Dab said. "How can you trust a pirate?"

"They know that the animals will keep an eye on them," Doctor Dolittle said.

All the pirates said, "We promise! We'll be farmers and live a quiet life!"

So the pirates—or new farmers—swam to shore. And Doctor Dolittle and his animals set sail once more.

CHAPTER 16

Too-Too the Listener

Doctor Dolittle and his animals headed off once more on their journey home.

Doctor Dolittle leaned on the rail at the back of the ship. He watched the Canary Islands fade away. He wondered how the monkeys were doing and what was happening in Puddleby-on-the-Marsh.

Dab-Dab ran up beside him. "Doctor Dolittle," he called. "This ship is beautiful! Have you looked around? It's really quite wonderful. The beds downstairs are made of silk. There are hundreds of pillows and cushions all over the room. There are soft, thick carpets. The dishes are made of silver. There are all sorts of wonderful things to eat, too."

"That does sound incredible," Doctor Dolittle said.

"There's also a locked room! It has a big heavy door with a large lock. Jip says that's where they must have kept all their treasure. You should come downstairs, Doctor," Dab-Dab said. "Maybe you can open the door."

So the doctor went downstairs. Dab-Dab was right. It was a beautiful ship. Doctor Dolittle had never been anywhere quite so lovely.

He found all the animals gathered around the locked door. They were all talking at once, trying to decide what was inside. The doctor turned the handle but it wouldn't open. They all searched the room for a key.

They lifted carpets and looked under chairs and tables. They looked in drawers and closets.

They discovered many wonderful things but not the key. So they all went back to stand by the door. Jip looked through the keyhole but could not see anything.

Then Too-Too said, "Wait, everyone! Please be still for a moment." They all stood quietly. "I think I hear someone inside the room."

They all listened again.

"I think you're mistaken," said Doctor Dolittle. "I don't hear anything."

"I'm sure of it!" the owl said. "Shhh! There it is again. Don't you hear that?"

The doctor and animals all shook their heads.

"I'm positive that I can hear someone putting his hand in his pocket," Too-Too said.

"That's so silly," Dab-Dab said. "How could you hear that? That makes almost no sound."

"I most certainly can hear that!" Too-Too said. "I could hear the sound a kitten makes when she shuts her eyes. I'm telling you, there's someone on the other side of this door putting his hand in his pocket!"

"Well then, what is happening now?" Doctor Dolittle asked.

"I'm not sure," Too-Too said. "Hold me up near the keyhole so I can hear more."

The doctor held lifted the owl up and held him close to the lock of the door.

After a moment or two, Too-Too said, "He's now rubbing his face with his left hand. It's a small hand and a small face. Now he's pushing his hair from his face."

"Is there anything else?" the doctor asked.

"He is sad. I can hear that he is weeping. He is being careful to not make any noise, but I can hear the tears fall."

"If the poor fellow is unhappy," said Doctor Dolittle, "we've got to get in and see what is the matter with him. Someone, quick! Find me an ax. I'll chop the door down!"

CHAPTER 17

The Ocean Gossips

‿༄

The animals quickly found an ax. Doctor Dolittle picked it up, took two heavy swings, and chopped a hole in the door. He made it just large enough to crawl through.

At first, the room was too dark to see anything. Doctor Dolittle lit a match.

The room was quite small. There were no windows and a low ceiling. There was only one small stool to sit on. In the middle of the floor sat a small boy crying bitterly. He was about eight years old.

The little boy was frightened by this man and all the strange animals. But as soon as he saw the doctor's face he stopped crying and stood up. "You're not one of the pirates, are you?" he said.

The doctor threw back his head and laughed. The little boy laughed, too.

"You have a very friendly laugh," the boy said. "Not like a pirate at all. I am worried, though. Have you seen my uncle?"

"Your uncle?" the Doctor said. "Was he on board this boat?"

"Yes," the boy said. There were tears in his eyes. "We were fishing together when the pirates caught us. They wanted my uncle to join them as a pirate. They took him away when he refused."

"And you have no idea what happened to him?" Doctor Dolittle asked.

"No," the boy cried. "They locked me in this room. I haven't been outside in more than a week! I asked them about my uncle but they wouldn't tell me anything. I'm so worried that he has drowned!"

"Try not to worry," Doctor Dolittle said. He patted the boy on his head. "We'll do everything we can to find your uncle."

"Oh, thank you!" he said.

"Could you describe your uncle for me?" Doctor Dolittle took out his notebook and pencil.

"Well, he is quite tall," the boy said. "And he has red hair. His boat was called the *Saucy Sally*. I have no idea what happened to it."

When he was finished, the boy took a nap in the sun. Doctor Dolittle went to the rail of the ship. He called out until a group of dolphins appeared at the side of the boat.

"I am looking for someone," he said. "Have you seen a tall fisherman with red hair? We think he has been missing for a week or two."

"Do you mean the owner of the *Saucy Sally*?"

one of the dolphins asked. "We've seen his boat. It's at the bottom of the sea. The fisherman isn't there, though. I can't say where he is, but he didn't drown."

"How can you say that for sure?" Doctor Dolittle asked.

"Oh, we would know," the dolphin answered. "They call us the ocean gossips because we know everything that happens in the water. If that fisherman drowned, we would know."

"Well, that's good news at least," the Doctor said. "I guess we'll have to keep looking. If you hear of anything, please let us know. His nephew is very worried."

The dolphins promised that they would.

Doctor Dolittle talked to the animals about forming a search party. Too-Too and Dab-Dab agreed to fly over the water to look for clues. The swallows said they would look, too.

"Remember to ask everyone you meet if they've seen a tall man with red hair," Doctor Dolittle said. "He must be somewhere!"

The other animals made sure the boy was happy while on the boat. They played games and ran along the deck. As you might imagine, the boy had never seen a pushmi-pullyu before. He wondered if he was seeing things!

The pushmi-pullyu did not mind being stared at by a child. He knew that the boy meant no harm. In fact, the pushmi-pullyu let the boy ride him around the boat!

Doctor Dolittle was quiet. He was worried about the boy's uncle. The doctor looked out over the water. He hoped they heard something very soon.

CHAPTER 18

Jip to the Rescue

❧

Dab-Dab and Too-Too knew they could not look everywhere. It would be hard even with the swallows' help. So Too-Too went to talk to the eagles. He found a black eagle, a bald eagle, and a golden eagle. They all agreed to fly over the jungles, forests, and mountains to look for the uncle.

The eagles returned to the boat the next day. "I'm sorry," the bald eagle said. "We didn't see the man you described. We'll keep our eye out, but I don't think he's anywhere on land."

Doctor Dolittle thanked the eagles for their help.

He shook his head. "I think I'm running out of ideas," he said. "I have no idea where to look now."

"Why don't you let me try," Jip said.

"You?" Dab-Dab said. "What can you do?"

"I might be able to find him by smell," Jip said.

"Oh, don't be ridiculous," Dab-Dab said. "We're in the middle of the ocean. You won't be able to smell anything out here!"

"You would be surprised," Jip said. He held his head high. He was not going to let a duck insult him. "Doctor Dolittle," the dog continued, "you could ask the boy if he has anything that belongs to his uncle."

Doctor Dolittle did as Jip asked. The boy gave him a gold ring on a string.

"My uncle handed it to me as soon as we saw the pirate ship," he said.

"No," Jip said to the doctor. "That won't do. Could you ask him if he has anything made of cloth?"

Once again Doctor Dolittle did as Jip asked. The boy handed the doctor a bright red bandanna.

"Perfect!" Jip said. "Now, if you just let me smell it . . ." Jip stuck his nose to the bandanna. He took many deep breaths.

"Don't worry, Doctor Dolittle," the dog said at last. "Please tell the boy that I will find his uncle. I'll definitely find his trail."

But it took several days. The problem was the wind. Jip could only smell scents that were blowing toward them. For the first few days, the wind was blowing from the east. Therefore, Jip could only smell things from that direction. Someone was making a lamb stew. Someone else was burning some leaves. However, there was no smell of the uncle.

Then one morning they woke up to winds from the west. Jip walked quickly to the railing on that side of the boat. He sniffed the air a few times, then called the doctor.

"I've got it!" he said. "I know where we should go."

"Really?" Doctor Dolittle said. "That's so exciting!"

"I'll stand at the front of the boat," Jip said. "Follow my nose as I sniff the air. We'll go straight to the uncle."

They did exactly as Jip asked. But instead of finding the uncle, they found a large rock. They sailed around and around it, but no one was there.

"I can smell him, though," Jip insisted. "He is definitely on that rock!"

One of the swallows flew over the rock. She went back and forth a few times. Then she hurried back to the boat. She told Doctor Dolittle that there was a large hole at the center of the rock.

"All right, then," he said. "We'll have to go ashore."

They anchored their boat by the rock, and Doctor Dolittle climbed out. He walked over to the hole. There was a long path leading inside. He lit a match and walked into the dark.

It took a moment for his eyes to adjust. At last he noticed something right in front of him. It took him a moment to realize what it was: the boy's uncle! He was sound asleep in the cave.

CHAPTER 19

Home

The boy and his uncle were very happy to see each other! The uncle picked his nephew up and gave him a big hug.

"What happened to you?" the boy asked.

"When I wouldn't join the pirates," his uncle began, "they left me on that rock all alone. I only had a little food and water. It's good that you found me when you did!"

"Yes, we're all very lucky," Doctor Dolittle agreed. "Now I think we should get you home. I'm sure everyone will be worried."

Doctor Dolittle followed the uncle's directions back to his home, where they arrived in only a few hours. Townsfolk ran to meet them as they docked in the harbor. As soon as they saw it was the little boy and his uncle, they began to cheer.

The townsfolk gathered around the boy. They listened as he told them what had happened. "If it weren't for Jip, we never would have found him!" he said.

A woman rushed through the crowd and grabbed the boy. She lifted him up into her arms. "My little boy!" she cried.

"Mother!" he said. He hugged her tight and began to cry.

The mayor of the town walked over to Doctor Dolittle. "How ever can we thank you?" he asked. "We surely would have lost them both without your help."

"We always help whenever we can," Doctor Dolittle said.

"Please stay for the night," the mayor said. "We'll have a feast and a dance to celebrate. It would be our honor."

So everyone walked back to the town. A long table was set up in the middle of the town square. They put up decorations and lit all the street lamps. Everyone brought food to share, so there was plenty to eat. They all sat down and had a wonderful meal.

After dinner, the mayor made a speech. He thanked Doctor Dolittle and the animals again. "And now we would like to give a present to Jip— something special for a special dog."

The mayor held out a small box. Doctor Dolittle opened it up for Jip. "My goodness," the doctor said. "How beautiful!" He held it out for Jip.

It was a collar made of solid gold, which read:

TO JIP: THE CLEVEREST DOG IN THE WORLD!

Jip wagged his tail to say "Thank you." He

asked Doctor Dolittle to pass the message on in human language, as well.

The celebration went long into the night. Everyone sang and danced and laughed. Doctor Dolittle could not remember the last time he'd had so much fun. And Jip could not remember a time when he'd felt so proud.

The next morning, Doctor Dolittle prepared to set sail again.

"Wouldn't you like to stay awhile longer?" the mayor asked.

"Yes," the boy added. "Why don't you stay until winter?"

"I'm sorry," Doctor Dolittle said. "I really must be going. I've been away for far too long already."

So the doctor and his animals all piled back on the boat. They set sail once again. All the towns-folk gathered on the beach and waved good-bye.

They arrived back in England on a bright sunny day. They did not go home right away, though. First of all, Doctor Dolittle sent the boat to his friend the fisherman. He hoped he would be pleased with the new pirate ship.

The pushmi-pullyu had grown to love the doctor and all the animals. He thought of them as his new family. He knew the doctor needed money to run his home. So the pushmi-pullyu told the doctor that would like to help. He offered to go on display.

"Are you sure?" the doctor asked. "I know you are shy. I don't want you feel uncomfortable."

"It would be my pleasure to help," the pushmi-pullyu said. "I don't feel so shy with all of you. I don't feel as lonely as I did in the jungle."

So the doctor and his animals toured the country. They stopped in every town along the way. They put up a sign that said:

SEE THE PUSHMI-PULLYU! ONLY FIFTY CENTS!

People came from miles around to see this strange creature.

They became so popular that they bought a tent, where more people could see the pushmi-pullyu at the same time. Of course, Doctor Dolittle let children in for free when he thought no one was looking. This made Dab-Dab angry but she did not try to stop it. How could she complain when it made the doctor so happy?

Eventually their show grew so well known that the men from the circus arrived. They wanted to buy the pushmi-pullyu. They offered Doctor Dolittle a great deal of money. It was enough that he would never have to worry again. But the doctor said no.

"I'm sorry, gentlemen," he said. "He is a friend of mine. I could never sell a friend. Besides, I promised to send him home if he was ever home-sick. How could I do that if he was in the circus?"

The circus men tried to change the doctor's mind. They offered him more money. They said he could visit whenever he wanted. But still the doctor said no.

When the leaves started to turn colors and the air was chilly, it was time to go home. Doctor Dolittle gathered his little troupe and headed back to Puddleby-on-the-Marsh.

Everything was fine at his home. The old horse had kept the place running smoothly. The house was clean and the yard was neat.

The horse had not done it all by himself, of course. The field mice and hedgehog helped out when they could. The fisherman and butcher also stopped by. They made sure there was enough straw and fresh water.

"Even your sister came to visit," the horse said. "She dusted the house and swept the floor. It was a great help."

"That was certainly kind of her," Doctor Dolittle said.

It was not long before everyone settled into old routines. Too-Too found his favorite place in the barn. Gub-Gub curled up in the corner of the yard. Dab-Dab made a nest for herself on the porch. Jip walked up and down the yard until he found the perfect tree to lie under. He was very proud of his gold collar. He showed it to everyone who stopped by.

Doctor Dolittle walked around his house. He looked through all his books and cupboards. It had been a wonderful adventure going to Africa but he was very, very glad to be home.

Back in Africa, the monkeys were doing much the same thing. Once the terrible sickness was over, they went back to their normal lives. They swung in trees and played in the fields. They ate bananas and green leaves.

At night, they told stories to one another, the same stories that Chee-Chee told Doctor Dolittle and the other animals about giant lizards and woolly mammoths. They also told stories about the great doctor who came to visit them when they were sick. The story of Doctor Dolittle was everyone's favorite.

"I wonder what the doctor is doing right now?" a little monkey asked.

"Do you think he'll come back to visit soon?" asked another.

Polynesia, who was staying with the monkeys, spoke up. "Of course he will!" she said. "I'm sure he will. How could he not come back for a visit? My word, monkeys can be very silly creatures!"

Then the crocodile would call up from his place by the river. "I'm sure he will! Now go to sleep!"

Even though they were thousands of miles apart, they still felt close to the doctor. They knew that he would always come if ever they needed him. All the animals lay their heads down and fell sound asleep, dreaming of their dear friend Doctor Dolittle back in Puddleby-on-the-Marsh.

What Do *You* Think?
Questions for Discussion

‿◌⁀

Have you ever been around a toddler who keeps asking the question "Why?" Does your teacher call on you in class with questions from your homework? Do your parents ask you questions about your day at the dinner table? We are always surrounded by questions that need a specific response. But is it possible to have a question with no right answer?

The following questions are about the book

you just read. But this is not a quiz! They are designed to help you look at the people, places, and events in the story from different angles. These questions do not have specific answers. Instead, they might make you think of the story in a completely new way.

Think carefully about each question and enjoy discovering more about this classic story.

1. Why does the butcher suggest that Doctor Dolittle become an animal doctor? Did you agree that this was a good idea? What do you want to be when you grow up?

2. Why does Sarah insist that Doctor Dolittle get rid of the crocodile? How does the doctor respond? What would you have done in his position?

3. How do Doctor Dolittle's animals pitch in around the house? Do you think the chores are properly assigned? What sort of chores do you have to do?

4. How does Doctor Dolittle learn of the monkeys' illness? What is the strangest message you've ever received?

5. Why does the little mouse hide away in Doctor Dolittle's luggage? Have you ever been on a voyage? Where would you most like to go?

6. How does Chee-Chee keep everyone amused while they are looking for the monkeys? Why does he know so many stories? How would you entertain the group?

7. Why do the monkeys decide to give Doctor Dolittle a going-away present? Do you think they decided on a good gift? What would you have given to the doctor?

8. How does Doctor Dolittle convince the prince that he has been transformed? Do you agree that you only need to believe in something for it to feel true? Have you ever believed in something enough to make it feel real?

9. How does Doctor Dolittle manage to get the pirate ship? Do you think it is right of him to take the boat? Have you ever taken something that didn't belong to you?

10. Doctor Dolittle says that there are all kinds of heroes. Do you agree? Is Doctor Dolittle a hero?

Afterword

by Arthur Pober, Ed.D.

෴

First impressions are important.

Whether we are meeting new people, going to new places, or picking up a book unknown to us, first impressions count for a lot. They can lead to warm, lasting memories or can make us shy away from any future encounters.

Can you recall your own first impressions and earliest memories of reading the classics?

Do you remember wading through pages and pages of text to prepare for an exam? Or were you the child who hid under the blanket to read with a flashlight, joining forces with Robin Hood to save Maid Marian? Do you remember only how long it took you to read a lengthy novel such as *Little Women*? Or did you become best friends with the March sisters?

Even for a gifted young reader, getting through long chapters with dense language can easily become overwhelming and can obscure the richness of the story and its characters. Reading an abridged, newly crafted version of a classic novel can be the gentle introduction a child needs to explore the characters and storyline without the frustration of difficult vocabulary and complex themes.

Reading an abridged version of a classic novel gives the young reader a sense of independence and the satisfaction of finishing a "grown-up" book. And when a child is engaged with and inspired by a classic story, the tone is set for further exploration of the story's themes, characters, history, and details. As a child's reading skills advance, the desire to tackle the original, unabridged version of the story will naturally emerge.

If made accessible to young readers, these stories can become invaluable tools for understanding themselves in the context of their families and social environments. This is why the Classic Starts series includes questions that stimulate discussion regarding the impact and social relevance of the characters and stories today. These questions can foster lively conversations between children and their parents or teachers. When we look at the issues, values, and standards of past times in terms of how we live now, we can appreciate literature's classic tales in a very personal and engaging way.

Share your love of reading the classics with a young child, and introduce an imaginary world real enough to last a lifetime.

Dr. Arthur Pober, Ed.D.

Dr. Arthur Pober has spent more than twenty years in the fields of early childhood and gifted education. He is the former principal of one of the world's oldest laboratory schools for gifted youngsters, Hunter College Elementary School, and former Director of Magnet Schools for the Gifted and Talented for more than 25,000 youngsters in New York City.

Dr. Pober is a recognized authority in the areas of media and child protection and is currently the U.S. representative to the European Institute for the Media and European Advertising Standards Alliance.

Explore these wonderful stories in our
Classic Starts™ library.

20,000 Leagues Under the Sea

The Adventures of Huckleberry Finn

The Adventures of Robin Hood

The Adventures of Sherlock Holmes

The Adventures of Tom Sawyer

Anne of Green Gables

Arabian Nights

Around the World in 80 Days

Black Beauty

The Call of the Wild

Dracula

Frankenstein

Gulliver's Travels

Heidi

The Hunchback of Notre-Dame